# Chai

# &

# code

## Prologue

Bangalore, the city of dreams and ambitions, where life's pace mirrors the buzz of the streets. Amidst this chaos, two individuals—Ravi and Ananya—strive to carve out their own paths in the relentless tech world. But life, much like the code they write, is full of bugs to fix, challenges to conquer, and fleeting moments of connection.

In this city that never sleeps, Ravi and Ananya embark on a journey of professional highs and personal struggles. As they navigate the demands of the tech industry, the story unfolds in a whirlwind of deadlines, teamwork, and growth—both in their careers and within themselves.

Life is not just about chasing success. It's about finding balance, cherishing the small moments, and learning to listen to the whispers of your heart amidst the noise. Their journey begins with an alarm ringing on a busy Bangalore morning, but where it will lead remains unknown, as they discover that every challenge is an opportunity in disguise.

# Contents

# Chapter 1: The Beginning of the Day

*"Life is a mosaic of moments; each day is a chance to add a vibrant tile."*

Ravi's alarm clock rang loudly, signalling the start of yet another busy day in Bangalore. He groggily reached out to turn it off, rubbing his eyes as he sat up in bed. "Another day, another line of code," he muttered to himself, stretching before heading to the bathroom. The sounds of the bustling city seeped through his windows: honking cars, street vendors calling out their wares, and the hum of morning traffic. After getting ready, he grabbed his bag and stepped out.

Ravi was a young software engineer, 26 years old, with a passion for coding and a mind always buzzing with ideas. His messy black hair and perpetually tired eyes were a testament to the long hours he spent in front of a computer screen. Despite the fatigue, there was a spark in his eyes, a sign of his unwavering determination and love for his work. Ravi had moved to Bangalore from his hometown in Kerala, chasing the dream of making it big in the tech industry. He often found solace in the chaos of the city, feeling at home amidst its vibrant energy and endless opportunities.

On the corner of MG Road, Ravi met Ananya, who was already there, sipping on a bottle of water and scrolling through her phone. Ananya was not just his best friend but also his closest confidant and colleague. She was 25, with sharp features and a brilliant mind. Her long hair was usually tied back in a neat ponytail, and her expressive brown eyes always seemed to be analysing everything around her.

Ananya had a knack for finding humour in the most mundane situations, often lightening the mood during their hectic workdays. She had moved to Bangalore from Chennai and quickly adapted to the city's fast-paced lifestyle. Ananya's parents were traditional, and though they supported her career, they often nudged her towards marriage and settling down, a topic that frequently amused and irritated her in equal measure.

"Good morning, Ananya! Ready for another day of coding and chaos?" Ravi asked with a smile, appreciating the familiar comfort of their morning routine.

Ananya looked up, returning his smile. "Morning, Ravi! You know it. Let's grab some tea from Manjunath's stall before heading in."

"Perfect idea. I need something to wake me up," Ravi agreed as they started walking down the bustling streets of Bangalore. The air was filled with the rich aroma of spices, street food, and the distinct scent of fresh tea brewing.

They arrived at Manjunath's tea stall, a small but popular spot among the locals. Manjunath, a middle-aged man with a warm smile, was busy preparing tea for his customers. He had been running this stall for over a decade, and his tea was legendary in the neighbourhood.

Manjunath was more than just a tea vendor; he was a friend and a confidant to many. He had seen the city change over the years and had countless stories to share. His wrinkled face and greying hair spoke of the many challenges he had faced, yet his eyes always twinkled with kindness and wisdom.

"Ravi, Ananya! The usual?" he asked, noticing them.

"Yes, Manjunath. One strong chai for me and a masala chai for Ananya," Ravi replied.

"Thanks, Manjunath. You always know how to make it just right," Ananya added.

Manjunath prepared their tea with practiced ease, his hands moving swiftly and surely. He poured the steaming tea into small clay cups and handed them over with a smile. "Anything for my regulars. So, what's new in the tech world?"

Ravi took a sip of his tea. "Same old, same old. Bugs and deadlines."

"But there's a big product launch coming up. We need all the energy we can get," Ananya chimed in.

Just then, Rashmi, a journalist, walked up to the stall. Rashmi was in her early 30s, with short, curly hair and an air of confidence. She had a reputation for being relentless in her pursuit of stories and had a keen eye for detail. Rashmi had grown up in Bangalore and had a deep love for the city, often writing about its many facets in her articles.

"Morning, everyone. Manjunath, can I get a black coffee?" she asked.

"Coming right up, Rashmi. How's the world of journalism treating you?" Manjunath replied, already starting to prepare her order.

"Busy as ever. There's a new development in the city's infrastructure project. Lots of stories to cover," Rashmi said with a sigh.

"Sounds exciting," Ravi remarked. "I'd trade debugging code for chasing stories any day."

"Trust me, it's not as glamorous as it sounds," Rashmi replied with a grin.

They chatted a bit more before finishing their tea and heading to the office. The day promised to be long and filled with challenges, but with good tea and great company, Ravi felt ready to tackle whatever came his way. The city was waking up, and so were its people, each with their own dreams and struggles, weaving the intricate tapestry of life in Bangalore.

*"In the hustle of city life, it's the small moments of connection that weave the strongest threads in the fabric of our days."*

# Chapter 2: At the Office

*"Every day is a new code to decipher, a fresh canvas to paint with our actions."*

Ravi and Ananya arrived at the sleek glass building that housed their office. The lobby was buzzing with employees, all hurrying to start their day. The air was filled with the soft hum of conversations and the clicking of keyboards, blending into a symphony of productivity. They made their way to their desks, exchanging greetings with their colleagues along the way.

Ravi's manager, Vikram, was already in the office, poring over a stack of documents. Vikram was in his mid-40s, with salt-and-pepper hair and a no-nonsense demeanour. He had a reputation for being tough but fair, and his deep-set eyes often carried a look of intense focus. Vikram had been a mentor to Ravi, guiding him through the intricacies of the tech world with patience and insight.

"Good morning, team. We have a lot to accomplish today," Vikram announced as Ravi and Ananya settled in.

"Morning, Vikram. Ready for the challenge," Ravi replied, his tone determined.

"Good morning, everyone. This is Nikhil, our new intern," Ananya introduced, gesturing to a nervous-looking young man standing beside her. Nikhil was fresh out of college, with an eager expression and a touch of anxiety in his eyes. His neatly combed hair and crisp shirt spoke of his desire to make a good impression.

"Hi, everyone. I'm excited to be here," Nikhil said, his voice a mix of enthusiasm and nervousness.

"Welcome, Nikhil. Don't worry, you'll fit right in," Priya assured him. Priya, a colleague and close friend of Ananya, was in her late 20s, with a warm smile and a reassuring presence. She had a knack for making newcomers feel at ease and was known for her collaborative spirit.

"Alright, let's get started. Ananya, you and Ravi will be leading the presentation tomorrow," Vikram instructed.

"Got it, Vikram. We'll make sure it's perfect," Ananya responded confidently.

As the team dispersed to their respective tasks, Ravi and Ananya sat down to discuss their strategy for the presentation. The room was filled with the low hum of conversations and the rhythmic tapping of keyboards. The office was a microcosm of Bangalore's vibrant energy, with its diverse mix of people and ideas coming together in a shared pursuit of innovation and success.

"Do you think we should include the latest user feedback in the presentation?" Ravi asked, scrolling through his laptop.

"Absolutely. It will show that we're listening to our users and constantly improving," Ananya replied, her eyes scanning through a list of recent updates.

Their conversation was interrupted by Priya, who approached their desk with a playful smile. "Hey, have you guys seen the latest office meme? It's hilarious," she said, holding up her phone.

Ravi chuckled as he glanced at the screen. "That's a good one. I needed that laugh."

"Me too," Ananya agreed. "Sometimes humour is the only thing that keeps us sane around here."

As the day progressed, the team worked diligently, their focus unwavering despite the occasional banter and shared jokes. Nikhil, though new, quickly found his rhythm, thanks to the supportive environment cultivated by his colleagues.

By late afternoon, the office was abuzz with anticipation for the upcoming presentation. Ravi and Ananya made final tweaks to their slides, ensuring every detail was perfect. The pressure was palpable, but so was the camaraderie. They knew they could count on each other to deliver.

"Feeling good about this?" Ravi asked, glancing at Ananya as they reviewed the final slide.

"Absolutely. We've got this," Ananya affirmed with a confident smile.

Just as they were about to wrap up, Vikram approached them, his expression one of approval. "Excellent work, both of you. I have no doubt tomorrow will be a success."

"Thanks, Vikram. We'll do our best," Ravi replied.

As the day came to a close, the office gradually emptied, with employees heading home to recharge for the challenges ahead. Ravi and Ananya lingered a bit longer, making sure everything was in place for the big day.

"Hey, Ravi. Want to grab dinner before heading home?" Ananya suggested.

"Sounds good. I could use a break," Ravi agreed.

They left the office together, stepping out into the cool evening air of Bangalore. The city was still alive with activity, its streets illuminated by the warm glow of streetlights. As they walked, they reflected on their journey so far and the many adventures that lay ahead.

*"In the tapestry of life, every thread of effort and moment of connection weaves a story worth telling."*

# Chapter 3: Dinner Conversations

*"In the quiet moments, we find the echoes of our deepest thoughts and dreams."*

Ravi and Ananya decided to dine at their favourite restaurant, a cozy place called "Southern Spice," known for its authentic South Indian cuisine. The warm, inviting atmosphere, coupled with the rich aroma of spices, provided a perfect backdrop for unwinding after a long day.

They settled into a corner table, and the waiter soon arrived with menus. "The usual for both of you?" he asked with a knowing smile.

"Yes, please," Ananya replied. "And maybe some vadas to start with."

As they waited for their food, they chatted about the day's events and the upcoming presentation. Ananya noticed that Ravi seemed more contemplative than usual.

"Hey, what's on your mind?" she asked, leaning forward slightly. "You seem a bit lost in thought."

Ravi sighed, running a hand through his hair. "It's just... sometimes I wonder if all this hard work is really worth it. I mean, we're constantly pushing ourselves, but at what cost? I barely have time for anything else."

Ananya nodded, understanding his sentiment. "I get it. It's easy to feel overwhelmed. But remember why we started this journey. We both wanted to create something meaningful, something that can make a difference."

Ravi smiled, appreciating her perspective. "You're right. It's just tough to keep that in mind when you're buried under deadlines."

Their conversation was momentarily interrupted as the waiter arrived with their food. The sight and smell of their favourite dishes lifted their spirits. The dosas were crispy and golden, the sambar fragrant and rich, and the vadas perfectly crunchy on the outside and soft inside.

As they dug in, Ananya decided to lighten the mood. "Do you remember our first project together? We were so clueless back then."

Ravi chuckled, recalling the memory. "Oh yeah, the infamous 'Chatbot Disaster.' We thought it would be a piece of cake, but it turned into a nightmare."

"We spent three nights straight trying to fix the bugs," Ananya added, laughing. "But we learned so much from that experience."

"And it brought us closer as a team," Ravi said, his mood lifting. "Those late-night coding sessions, the endless cups of coffee... It's all part of the journey."

Ananya nodded, smiling warmly. "Exactly. Every challenge has shaped us into who we are today. And we've had some great moments along the way."

Their conversation shifted to lighter topics as they continued their meal, sharing stories and laughing over past mishaps. The bond they shared was evident in their easy camaraderie, their mutual respect and understanding.

After dinner, they decided to take a walk around the nearby park. The evening air was cool and refreshing, a welcome contrast to the hustle of the day. The park was relatively quiet, with only a few people strolling or sitting on benches, enjoying the serene atmosphere.

As they walked, Ananya spoke about her family. "My parents called today. They're coming to visit next month. You know how they are—always worried about my well-being."

Ravi smiled. "They just care about you. It's nice to have family who's concerned."

"True," Ananya agreed. "But sometimes it feels like they're trying to plan every aspect of my life. I love them, but I wish they'd trust my decisions more."

"I think they do, in their own way," Ravi said thoughtfully. "It's just hard for them to let go. You're their little girl, after all."

Ananya laughed. "I suppose you're right. How about you? Any updates from your family?"

"Yeah, I talked to my mom yesterday," Ravi replied. "She's always asking when I'll visit. I miss them, but work keeps me so busy."

"Maybe you should take a break and go home for a few days," Ananya suggested. "It might do you some good."

"Maybe," Ravi said, considering the idea. "It's been a while since I had a proper break."

As they made their way back to the main road, Ravi felt a renewed sense of purpose. Talking with Ananya always had a way of putting things into perspective. They were in this together, facing the highs and lows as a team.

When they reached the point where their paths diverged, Ananya turned to him. "Thanks for tonight, Ravi. I really needed this."

"Me too," Ravi replied. "See you tomorrow. Let's crush that presentation."

"Absolutely," Ananya said with a grin. "Good night."

"Good night," Ravi echoed, watching her walk away before heading to his apartment.

The city lights shimmered around him, and he felt a sense of belonging. Bangalore was more than just a city; it was a canvas where he and Ananya were painting their dreams, one brushstroke at a time.

*"True friendships are the anchors that keep us grounded amidst the storms of life."*

# Chapter 4: The Big Presentation

*"Every step forward is a testament to our courage and a beacon for our dreams."*

The morning of the presentation dawned bright and early. Ravi woke up with a sense of anticipation and a hint of nervous excitement. This was a big day for him and Ananya, a culmination of weeks of hard work. He got ready quickly, dressed in his best formal attire, and made sure to review the presentation one last time before heading out.

At the office, the atmosphere was charged with energy. Colleagues moved with purpose, preparing for the day's events. Ravi met Ananya at her desk, and they exchanged determined smiles. She looked confident in her professional attire, her hair neatly tied back, and her demeanour calm and focused.

"Ready to rock this?" Ananya asked, her eyes sparkling with excitement.

"Absolutely. Let's show them what we've got," Ravi replied, feeling a surge of confidence.

They headed to the conference room where the presentation was to be held. It was a spacious room with a large screen, sleek chairs, and a polished wooden table. The company's leadership team was already gathered, including Vikram, who gave them an encouraging nod.

The room filled quickly with colleagues and stakeholders, all eager to see the new product. Ravi and Ananya set up their laptops, making sure everything was in order. As the chatter died down, Vikram stood up to introduce them.

"Good morning, everyone. Today, Ravi and Ananya will be presenting our latest product. This project has been a significant effort, and I have no doubt it will be a game-changer for us," Vikram began, his voice steady and confident.

Ravi felt a brief moment of anxiety but took a deep breath, reminding himself of their preparation. Ananya started the presentation with an engaging introduction, smoothly transitioning into the core features of the product. She highlighted the key benefits, demonstrating how it addressed user needs and outperformed competitors. Ravi took over, delving into the technical details. He explained the innovative aspects of the design, using diagrams and flowcharts to illustrate complex concepts. His passion for the project shone through, capturing the audience's attention.

"By integrating AI-driven algorithms, we've significantly improved user experience. Our testing shows a 40% increase in efficiency, which is a substantial leap from our previous version," Ravi explained, his voice clear and confident.

As they moved through the presentation, they could see the positive reactions from their audience. Heads nodded in approval, and there were occasional murmurs of appreciation. When they finished, the room erupted in applause.

"Well done, both of you," Vikram said, standing up to shake their hands. "This is impressive work, and I'm confident it will be a great success."

"Thank you, Vikram. We're excited about the possibilities," Ananya replied, beaming with pride.

After the presentation, colleagues came up to congratulate them. Nikhil, the new intern, looked especially inspired. "That was amazing! I hope I can contribute like that someday," he said, his eyes wide with admiration.

"You will, Nikhil. Just keep learning and stay passionate," Ravi encouraged, patting him on the back.

The rest of the day felt lighter, the weight of the presentation lifted from their shoulders. Ravi and Ananya decided to celebrate their success with a small team lunch. They headed to a nearby café, a cozy spot with outdoor seating and a relaxed atmosphere.

As they sat down, Priya joined them, bringing her usual cheerful energy. "You guys were fantastic! I knew you'd nail it," she said, raising her glass of iced tea in a toast.

"Thanks, Priya. It feels great to see our hard work pay off," Ananya replied, clinking her glass with Priya's.

They ordered a variety of dishes, from spicy paneer tikka to creamy butter chicken, enjoying the delicious food and each other's company. The conversation flowed easily, filled with laughter and shared memories.

"So, what's next for you two?" Priya asked, her eyes twinkling with curiosity.

"Well, we have a few more projects in the pipeline, but for now, I think we deserve a little break," Ravi said, leaning back in his chair with a satisfied smile.

Ananya nodded in agreement. "Absolutely. Maybe even a short vacation. We've earned it."

As they finished their meal, Ravi looked around at his friends, feeling a deep sense of gratitude. Despite the challenges and the long hours, moments like these made it all worthwhile. They were not just colleagues; they were a team, a family, united by their shared dreams and efforts.

Walking back to the office, Ravi felt a renewed sense of purpose. The journey was far from over, but with friends like Ananya and Priya by his side, he knew he could face whatever came next.

*"In the symphony of life, it's the harmonious blend of effort and support that creates the most beautiful melodies."*

## Chapter 5: New Beginnings

*"In the ever-turning wheel of life, every ending is just a prelude to a new beginning."*

The successful presentation had given Ravi and Ananya a newfound confidence and a sense of accomplishment. The weeks that followed were a whirlwind of positive feedback and exciting new opportunities. The product launch was a success, and the team's hard work was paying off. The office buzzed with activity as they worked on enhancing the product based on user feedback and planning future projects.

One morning, Ravi received a call from his mother. "Ravi, when are you coming home? We miss you," she said, her voice warm and familiar. Ravi felt a pang of guilt. It had been months since his last visit. "I know, Amma. Work has been so hectic. But things are settling down now, so I'll plan a visit soon."

"You should. We have so much to catch up on," she replied, her tone brightening.

After the call, Ravi found himself lost in thought. He missed his family and the comfort of home. He decided it was time for a short break and discussed it with Ananya and Vikram.

"Go for it, Ravi," Ananya said. "You deserve some time off. We can manage here."

Vikram agreed. "Take a week off, Ravi. Family is important, and you've earned it."

With their support, Ravi booked his tickets to Kerala. The thought of seeing his family and revisiting his hometown filled him with a sense of nostalgia and excitement.

The following week, Ravi boarded a train to Kerala. As the train chugged along, he watched the changing landscapes, the bustling cities giving way to the serene countryside. The lush greenery and the scent of fresh rain brought back memories of his childhood. He felt a wave of calm wash over him, a stark contrast to the fast-paced life in Bangalore.

Upon reaching his hometown, Ravi was greeted by his parents at the station. Their faces lit up with joy as they embraced him. "Welcome home, son," his father said, his voice filled with pride.

"It's so good to see you, Amma, Appa," Ravi said, his heart swelling with affection.

The days that followed were filled with laughter, family meals, and long conversations. Ravi cherished the simplicity of home—the morning coffee on the veranda, the home-cooked meals, and the familiar faces of neighbours. He felt a renewed sense of connection with his roots.

One evening, as he sat with his father on the veranda, they talked about life and work. "I'm proud of you, Ravi. You've achieved so much," his father said, his voice steady and reassuring.

"Thanks, Appa. But sometimes it feels like I'm constantly chasing something. I miss the peace of this place," Ravi confessed.

"Balance is key, son. It's important to strive for your dreams, but also to find time for yourself and your loved ones," his father advised.

Ravi nodded, reflecting on his father's words. He realized that while ambition drove him, it was equally important to pause and appreciate the journey.

As his visit came to an end, Ravi felt a mix of emotions. He was grateful for the time spent with his family and the clarity it brought him. He promised himself to maintain a better balance between work and personal life.

Back in Bangalore, Ravi was greeted with enthusiasm by his colleagues. "Welcome back! How was your trip?" Ananya asked, her eyes sparkling with curiosity.

"It was wonderful. Just what I needed," Ravi replied, feeling rejuvenated.

They quickly caught up on work, diving back into their projects with renewed Vigor. The office felt like a second home, a place where they could pursue their dreams together.

One evening, after a particularly productive day, Ravi and Ananya decided to take a walk around the nearby park. The sky was painted with hues of orange and pink as the sun set, casting a warm glow over the city.

"Ananya, have you ever thought about what you really want out of life?" Ravi asked, breaking the comfortable silence.

Ananya pondered the question. "I think I want to make a difference, to create something meaningful. But I also want to find happiness and balance. It's a tough mix to achieve."

"Yeah, I get that," Ravi agreed. "I realized during my visit home that while our work is important, it's also crucial to find joy in the little things and cherish the people we love."

Ananya smiled. "Wise words, Ravi. I think we're on the right path, and as long as we support each other, we'll find our way."

As they walked, the city lights began to twinkle, reflecting the endless possibilities that lay ahead. They felt a renewed sense of purpose, ready to face the future with determination and hope.

*"The journey is as important as the destination, and the moments we share along the way are the true treasures of life."*

# Chapter 6: New Challenges

*"Embrace the unknown, for it holds the seeds of growth and transformation."*

The buzz from the successful product launch had settled, and the office atmosphere had returned to its usual rhythm. However, it wasn't long before new challenges emerged. The company was preparing to expand its reach, aiming to penetrate the international market. This ambitious goal required innovative solutions and exceptional teamwork.

Ravi and Ananya were called into a meeting with Vikram to discuss the new project. Vikram's office, with its large windows offering a panoramic view of Bangalore's skyline, was a testament to the company's growth and aspirations.

"Good morning, Ravi, Ananya," Vikram greeted them, motioning for them to sit. "We have an exciting but demanding project ahead. Our goal is to adapt our product for the international market. This means addressing different user requirements, regulations, and cultural nuances."

Ravi and Ananya exchanged glances; their excitement tempered by the gravity of the task. "We're up for the challenge, Vikram," Ravi said, his voice steady.

"Excellent, we'll be assembling a specialized team for this project. You two will lead it," Vikram continued. "We'll also be collaborating with teams from our offices abroad, so communication and coordination will be key."

As they left Vikram's office, the weight of the responsibility began to settle in. "This is huge, Ravi," Ananya said, her voice tinged with both excitement and apprehension.

"Yeah, it is. But we've handled tough projects before. We can do this," Ravi replied, trying to reassure both himself and Ananya.

They spent the next few days selecting team members for the project. They chose a mix of experienced developers and fresh talent, including Nikhil, whose enthusiasm and quick learning had impressed them. Priya was also part of the team, bringing her valuable insights and collaborative spirit.

The first team meeting was a mix of introductions and strategic discussions. Ravi and Ananya outlined the project goals and timelines, emphasizing the importance of innovation and teamwork. The team members, each bringing their unique skills and perspectives, were eager to dive into the project.

As the weeks progressed, the team faced numerous challenges. Adapting the product for different markets was a complex task, requiring thorough research and constant adjustments. There were late nights and intense brainstorming sessions, but the team's dedication never wavered.

One evening, after a particularly gruelling day, Ravi and Ananya decided to grab dinner at a nearby café. The cozy ambiance and delicious food provided a much-needed break from the relentless pace of work.

"This project is testing us in ways we didn't anticipate," Ananya said, stirring her cup of coffee. "But it's also pushing us to think outside the box."

"True," Ravi agreed, taking a sip of his drink. "I think the key is to stay flexible and open to new ideas. We're in uncharted territory, but that's where the real growth happens."

Ananya nodded thoughtfully. "Speaking of growth, I've been thinking about how this project is changing us—not just professionally, but personally too. We're learning to navigate new cultures, adapt to different working styles, and communicate more effectively."

"Absolutely. It's a steep learning curve, but it's making us better leaders," Ravi said, feeling a sense of pride in their progress.

As they continued their conversation, they realized how much they had evolved since they first started working together. The challenges they faced were forging them into a stronger, more cohesive team.

Back at the office, the team's hard work began to show results. They successfully adapted the product for the first international market, receiving positive feedback from the overseas team. The sense of accomplishment was palpable, but there was still much to do.

One afternoon, Priya approached Ravi with a concerned look. "Ravi, I've been reviewing our recent data, and I think we might need to rethink our approach for the European market. The user behaviour is quite different from what we expected."

Ravi frowned, examining the data Priya had compiled. "You're right. This is significant. Let's call a team meeting and brainstorm possible solutions."

The meeting room buzzed with ideas and discussions. The team debated various strategies, weighing the pros and cons of each approach. Nikhil, despite being the youngest and least experienced, offered a fresh perspective that sparked a breakthrough.

"What if we focus more on user personalization? Tailoring the experience based on user preferences could address the differences in behaviour," Nikhil suggested.

The team pondered his idea, and slowly, a plan began to take shape. They decided to implement a more personalized approach, incorporating feedback and testing it rigorously.

As the project continued, Ravi and Ananya found themselves growing not just as professionals, but as individuals. They learned to embrace uncertainty, to lead with empathy, and to find strength in their team's diversity.

One evening, as they wrapped up another productive day, Ravi turned to Ananya. "I think we're not just building a product here. We're building something bigger—a team that can tackle any challenge, a network of support that goes beyond work."

Ananya smiled, her eyes reflecting the same realization. "You're right, Ravi. This project is more than just a milestone in our careers. It's a journey of growth, resilience, and camaraderie."

*"Challenges are the crucible in which our true strengths are forged, and our greatest growth is realized."*

# Chapter 7: Crossroads

*"In every decision lies the potential for transformation; it is the choices we make that define our path."*

The months that followed were a blur of meetings, deadlines, and endless problem-solving sessions. The international expansion project was progressing well, but it was also taking a toll on everyone. The team's hard work was paying off, but the constant pressure was beginning to show.

One evening, Ravi received a call from his friend and former college roommate, Karthik. They hadn't spoken in months, and Ravi was delighted to hear from him.

"Hey, Ravi! Long time no talk. How are things?" Karthik's voice was cheerful, a stark contrast to Ravi's exhaustion.

"Hey, Karthik! It's been crazy busy here. How about you?" Ravi replied, sinking into his couch.

"Same here, but I've got some exciting news. I've been offered a position in a start-up in Hyderabad. They're working on some cutting-edge AI tech, and they want me to join their core team."

"Wow, that's amazing! Congratulations!" Ravi exclaimed, genuinely happy for his friend.

"Thanks, man. Actually, I was calling to see if you might be interested in joining us. We need someone with your skills and experience. The opportunity is incredible, and I think you'd love the challenge."

Ravi was taken aback. The idea of a new opportunity was both thrilling and daunting.

"That sounds tempting, Karthik. But I'm so invested in the current project here. It would be tough to leave."

"I get it. Just think about it. Sometimes a change can be good," Karthik said, his tone understanding.

After they hung up, Ravi sat in silence, his mind racing. The offer was enticing, but it also meant leaving behind the team and the work they had poured their hearts into. He decided to talk it over with Ananya.

The next morning, Ravi and Ananya met for coffee before heading to the office. Ananya could tell something was on Ravi's mind. "You seem preoccupied. What's up?" she asked, taking a sip of her coffee.

Ravi hesitated before sharing Karthik's offer. "I got a call from Karthik last night. He's joining a start-up in Hyderabad and offered me a position there. It's a great opportunity, but I don't know if I should leave."

Ananya's eyes widened in surprise. "Wow, that's a big decision. How do you feel about it?"

"I'm torn. The start-up sounds exciting, but I feel a sense of loyalty to our team here. We've built so much together," Ravi confessed.

Ananya nodded, understanding his dilemma. "It's a tough choice. You need to think about what you really want, both professionally and personally."

Ravi appreciated her support. "Thanks, Ananya. I'll give it some serious thought."

As the days passed, Ravi found himself increasingly distracted. He continued to lead the team with Ananya, but the decision weighed heavily on him. He spent long nights pondering his future, torn between the familiarity of his current job and the allure of a new adventure.

One evening, Ravi decided to visit his favourite spot in Bangalore—a quiet hilltop that offered a panoramic view of the city. It was a place he often went to when he needed to clear his mind. As he sat there, watching the city lights twinkle below, he reflected on his journey so far.

He thought about the challenges they had overcome, the friendships they had forged, and the growth he had experienced. He realized that his decision wasn't just about career advancement; it was about what truly made him happy.

The next day, Ravi called Karthik. "Hey, Karthik. I've thought about your offer, and it's a fantastic opportunity. But I've decided to stay here.

There's still so much I want to accomplish with my current team."

Karthik was supportive. "I respect your decision, Ravi. You have to follow your heart. We'll always have opportunities to collaborate in the future."

Feeling a sense of clarity and peace, Ravi returned to the office. He gathered the team and shared his thoughts. "I want to let you all know that I had an opportunity to join a start-up in Hyderabad. It was a tough decision, but I've decided to stay here and continue our journey together."

The team responded with smiles and nods of approval. Ananya, especially, looked relieved. "We're glad you're staying, Ravi. We have a lot more to achieve together."

With renewed focus, Ravi and Ananya led the team through the next phase of the project. The challenges were still there, but so was their determination and unity. They worked tirelessly, driven by a shared vision and the knowledge that they were stronger together.

*"In the tapestry of life, it is the threads of loyalty and perseverance that create the most enduring patterns."*

# Chapter 8: The Turning Point

*"Every challenge is an opportunity in disguise, waiting to reveal a new horizon."*

With Ravi's decision to stay, the team felt a renewed sense of purpose and commitment. The international expansion project was entering its critical phase, and every member was giving their all. The office hummed with activity, the air thick with a mixture of tension and excitement.

One morning, Ravi and Ananya were called into Vikram's office for a progress review. Vikram's serious expression hinted at the importance of the meeting.

"Good morning, Ravi, Ananya," Vikram began, gesturing for them to sit. "I've been reviewing our progress, and while we're making significant strides, we've hit a few snags that could jeopardize our timeline."

Ananya leaned forward; her brow furrowed. "What kind of snags, Vikram?"

"Primarily, it's about localization issues. We're not just translating the product; we need to ensure it aligns with local regulations and cultural expectations. Our initial approach isn't as effective as we hoped," Vikram explained.

Ravi felt a knot tighten in his stomach. "Do we have any specific feedback on where we're falling short?"

Vikram nodded, passing them a report. "We've received detailed feedback from our European partners. I need you both to lead the charge in addressing these concerns. We have a tight deadline to meet."

Leaving Vikram's office, Ravi and Ananya exchanged glances. The stakes were high, but they were determined to find a solution. They gathered the team for an emergency meeting to discuss the new developments.

"Alright, everyone," Ravi began, his tone serious. "We've got some challenges to overcome with our localization efforts. We need to rethink our approach and come up with solutions fast."

The room was silent for a moment before Priya spoke up. "I think we need to bring in some local experts who understand the nuances we're missing. Maybe consultants from the regions we're targeting."

"That's a great idea," Ananya agreed. "We should also consider forming small sub-teams focused on specific regions. This way, we can tailor our efforts more effectively."

Nikhil, always eager, added, "We can also use AI to analysed regional user data more effectively. It can help us identify patterns and preferences that we might be overlooking."

Ravi nodded, appreciating the proactive suggestions. "Let's implement these ideas. I'll handle reaching out to consultants, and Ananya can oversee the formation of regional sub-teams. Nikhil, start working on the data analysis."

As the team dispersed to tackle their tasks, Ravi felt a sense of determination. They had faced challenges before, and he was confident in their ability to overcome this one.

Over the next few weeks, the office transformed into a hive of focused activity. Consultants from Europe and Asia joined the team, providing invaluable insights. The sub-teams worked diligently, tailoring the product to meet regional needs. Nikhil's AI-driven analysis yielded crucial data, helping them refine their strategies.

One evening, as the team worked late, Ravi noticed Ananya staring intently at her screen. "What's on your mind, Ananya?" he asked, pulling up a chair next to her.

Ananya sighed, rubbing her temples. "It's just... there's so much to consider. Every time we solve one issue, another pops up. It feels like an endless cycle."

Ravi placed a reassuring hand on her shoulder. "I know it's tough. But remember, we've always found a way through. This time won't be any different."

Ananya smiled faintly. "Thanks, Ravi. I needed that. Let's keep pushing forward."

The turning point came one late night when Nikhil burst into the office with a breakthrough.

"Guys, you need to see this!" he exclaimed, waving a stack of printouts.

Everyone gathered around as Nikhil explained his findings. "The AI analysis has identified a key user behaviour trend we missed.

If we adjust our user interface to match these preferences, it could significantly improve our product's reception in Europe."

Excitement buzzed in the room as they reviewed the data. "This is exactly what we needed," Ananya said, her eyes lighting up. "Let's implement these changes immediately."

Over the next few days, the team worked tirelessly to incorporate the new insights. The atmosphere in the office shifted from one of anxiety to one of hopeful determination. When they finally sent the updated product to them

European partners, there was a collective sense of anticipation.

A week later, they received the feedback. It was overwhelmingly positive. The adjustments had hit the mark, addressing the concerns and exceeding expectations. The team's hard work had paid off.

Ravi and Ananya called a team meeting to share the good news. "Everyone, we did it!" Ravi announced, his voice filled with pride. "Our partners are thrilled with the updates. This is a major win for us."

The room erupted in cheers and applause. It was a moment of triumph, a testament to their resilience and teamwork.

Later, as they celebrated with a team dinner, Ravi felt a deep sense of gratitude. "This project has been one of the toughest, but also one of the most rewarding," he said, raising his glass. "To our team, for never giving up and always pushing forward. Cheers!"

"Cheers!" the team echoed, clinking glasses.

As the evening progressed, Ravi and Ananya found a quiet corner to reflect on their journey. "We've come a long way, haven't we?" Ananya said, her eyes reflecting the city lights.

"Yes, we have," Ravi agreed. "And I think this is just the beginning. There are still many challenges ahead, but with a team like ours, I know we can overcome anything."

*"Success is not the absence of challenges, but the mastery of perseverance and adaptation."*

# Chapter 9: Personal Sacrifices

*"In the pursuit of dreams, personal sacrifices pave the way to greater triumphs."*

With the success of their international expansion, the team at Infinite Innovations was riding a high wave of morale. The office was abuzz with excitement, and the sense of accomplishment was palpable. However, the intense workload and long hours began to take a toll on their personal lives, leading to moments of introspection and difficult decisions.

Ravi found himself reflecting on his life outside of work. The long hours at the office meant he was often too tired to catch up with friends or pursue his hobbies. One evening, while going through some old photos, he stumbled upon a picture of himself with his college friends at a music festival. It was a stark reminder of the vibrant life he once led, filled with laughter, music, and spontaneous adventures.

That weekend, Ravi decided to reconnect with his old friends. He called up Karthik, who was now busy with his start-up in Hyderabad, and arranged a video call with their other college mates. As they caught up, Ravi realized how much he had missed these simple moments of camaraderie.

"We need to meet up soon," Karthik suggested. "It's been too long."

Ravi agreed. "Absolutely. Let's plan something. I could use a break."

Meanwhile, Ananya was grappling with her own set of challenges. Her parents had been hinting at marriage, and the topic had become a frequent point of contention. Balancing the demands of her career with family expectations was proving to be a delicate act.

One evening, Ananya's mother called. "Ananya, we need to talk. Your father and I are concerned about your future. Have you given any thought to settling down?"

Ananya sighed, feeling the familiar pressure. "Amma, I'm focused on my career right now. This project is very important to me."

"I understand, but life is more than just work. We want to see you happy and settled," her mother insisted.

"I know, Amma. But please give me some time. I need to figure things out," Ananya replied, trying to keep her frustration in check.

At the office, Ravi noticed Ananya's distracted demeanour. "Is everything okay, Ananya?" he asked one afternoon.

Ananya hesitated before opening up. "It's my parents. They're pressuring me about marriage. It's just... a lot to handle on top of everything else."

Ravi nodded sympathetically. "I get it. Balancing personal and professional life is tough. If you need to talk or take some time, I'm here."

"Thanks, Ravi. I appreciate it," Ananya said, feeling a bit lighter.

As the weeks went by, the pressure intensified. The team was gearing up for the next major phase of their project—launching in the American market. This required even more dedication and late nights. Ravi and Ananya often found themselves staying at the office long after everyone else had left.

One particularly late night, Ravi and Ananya sat in the conference room, surrounded by documents and empty coffee cups. The city outside was quiet, a stark contrast to the whirlwind of activity inside.

"Do you ever wonder if all these sacrifices are worth it?" Ananya asked, breaking the silence.

Ravi looked up from his laptop, contemplating her question. "Sometimes, yes. But then I think about what we're building, the impact we're making. It keeps me going."

Ananya nodded. "I feel the same way. But I can't help but worry about missing out on other aspects of life."

Ravi smiled, a hint of sadness in his eyes. "It's a tough balance. We just have to hope that in the end, it's all worth it."

Their conversation was interrupted by a message from Vikram, asking for an update on the project's progress. It was a reminder of the relentless pace they had to maintain.

Despite the personal challenges, the team continued to push forward. They knew that their hard work was laying the foundation for something significant. However, the sacrifices they were making became more evident with each passing day.

One weekend, Ravi decided to visit his parents in Kerala. The trip home was a much-needed respite from the constant grind. As he sat with his father, discussing life and work, Ravi felt a sense of clarity.

"Appa, do you think I'm making the right choices?" Ravi asked, his voice filled with uncertainty.

His father smiled, placing a reassuring hand on his shoulder. "Ravi, life is about making choices and accepting the consequences. You're following your passion, and that's important. But don't forget to take care of yourself and cherish the moments with those you love."

Ravi nodded, feeling a renewed sense of purpose. His father's words resonated deeply, reminding him of the importance of balance.

Back in Bangalore, Ananya had a heart-to-heart with her mother. They talked about her career, her dreams, and the pressures she felt.

By the end of the conversation, there was a newfound understanding between them.

"Ananya, we just want you to be happy. Take your time and follow your heart," her mother said, her voice gentle.

"Thank you, Amma. I promise I'll find a way to balance everything," Ananya replied, feeling a weight lift off her shoulders.

As Ravi and Ananya returned to the office, they carried with them the lessons learned from their personal journeys. They were more determined than ever to make their project a success, but they also understood the importance of maintaining their personal well-being.

*"True success is not just about achieving goals but also about finding harmony in the chaos and nurturing the relationships that matter most."*

# Chapter 10: A Heartbeat Away

*"In the quiet moments, the heart often whispers the truths the mind has yet to understand."*

With the American market launch looming, the intensity in the office reached a fever pitch. Each day brought new challenges, but also the thrill of progress. The team was united in their mission, working seamlessly together, yet the strain of the continuous hustle began to weigh on everyone, especially Ravi and Ananya.

One late evening, the office was eerily quiet except for the faint hum of computers and the occasional shuffle of papers. Ravi and Ananya were the last ones left, as usual, engrossed in a discussion about the latest user interface design. They had just implemented Nikhil's AI-driven suggestions and were eager to see the results.

"Do you think this will finally crack the user engagement issue?" Ananya asked, rubbing her eyes.

Ravi leaned back in his chair, staring at the ceiling. "I hope so. It's our best shot yet. If we can get this right, the launch will be a huge success."

Ananya nodded, though her mind was elsewhere. She had been feeling increasingly overwhelmed, the constant pressure gnawing at her. She knew Ravi was feeling it too, though he rarely showed it.

"Ravi," Ananya said softly, breaking the silence.

"Do you ever feel like we're losing ourselves in all of this? The project, the deadlines... it's like we're running on autopilot."

Ravi turned to look at her, his expression thoughtful. "Yeah, I do. Sometimes I wonder if we're missing out on the bigger picture, the things that truly matter."

Their conversation was interrupted by the sudden ringing of Ravi's phone. It was his mother. He answered, his voice a mix of surprise and concern.

"Amma, is everything okay?"

"Ravi, your father had a heart attack. He's in the hospital," his mother's voice trembled with fear and worry.

Ravi's world tilted on its axis. "I'm coming home right away, Amma. Don't worry."

He hung up, his hands shaking. "Ananya, I have to go. My father... he's in the hospital."

Ananya's eyes widened in shock. "Go, Ravi. Don't worry about anything here. I'll manage. Just go and take care of your family."

Ravi nodded, grateful for her understanding. He left the office in a rush, his mind a whirlwind of fear and worry.

The journey back to Kerala felt like an eternity. When Ravi finally arrived at the hospital, he found his mother in the waiting room, her face etched with anxiety. She embraced him tightly, and for a moment, Ravi allowed himself to feel the weight of his emotions.

"How is he, Amma?" Ravi asked, his voice barely a whisper.

"The doctors said it was a mild heart attack. He's stable now, but they need to keep him under observation," his mother explained, her eyes glistening with unshed tears.

Ravi nodded, a mix of relief and concern flooding through him. He sat by his father's bedside, holding his hand, feeling a deep sense of vulnerability. It was a stark reminder of the fragility of life and the importance of family.

Back in Bangalore, Ananya was doing her best to hold the fort. She informed the team about Ravi's situation, and everyone rallied together to support him in his absence. They worked tirelessly, determined to ensure the project stayed on track.

During one of their late-night sessions, Ananya received a message from her parents. They had arranged a meeting with a prospective groom's family, despite her repeated pleas for more time. She felt a surge of frustration and helplessness. Torn between her responsibilities at work and the expectations of her family, Ananya felt like she was on the brink of breaking.

That night, after the team had left, Ananya stayed behind, feeling the weight of her personal and professional struggles. She wandered into the break room, where she found Nikhil, who had also stayed late to finish some work.

"Hey, Ananya," Nikhil said, looking up from his laptop. "You, okay? You look like you've got the world on your shoulders."

Ananya managed a weak smile. "Just a lot going on. My parents are pressuring me about marriage again. And with Ravi gone, the project feels even more overwhelming."

Nikhil nodded sympathetically. "I can't imagine how tough that must be. But you're doing an incredible job, Ananya. We all see how hard you're working. And Ravi's dad will be okay. He's in good hands."

Ananya sighed, feeling a little comforted by Nikhil's words. "Thanks, Nikhil. Sometimes it just feels like too much."

"I know. But you're not alone in this. We're all here for you," Nikhil said, giving her a reassuring smile.

The next morning, Ravi called Ananya to give her an update. "My dad is doing better. They're keeping him for a few more days, but he's out of danger."

"That's a relief, Ravi. Take all the time you need. We've got things covered here," Ananya replied, her voice steady.

"Thanks, Ananya. I'll be back as soon as I can," Ravi said, feeling a wave of gratitude for his supportive team.

Over the next few days, Ananya and the team pushed forward with the project. They encountered several challenges, but with each obstacle, they grew stronger and more cohesive. Ananya found solace in the unity and determination of her colleagues, who worked tirelessly to ensure the success of the American market launch.

When Ravi returned to Bangalore, he was greeted with a mix of relief and gratitude. The team had not only managed in his absence but had made significant progress. Ravi felt a renewed sense of purpose and commitment, knowing that they could rely on each other no matter what.

One evening, after a particularly productive day, Ravi and Ananya took a moment to reflect on their journey. They sat on the office terrace, overlooking the city lights.

"Ravi, I've realized something," Ananya said, breaking the silence. "No matter how tough things get, we always find a way through. It's our resilience and the support of our team that makes it possible."

Ravi nodded; his heart full of appreciation. "You're right, Ananya. We're stronger together. And as long as we remember what truly matters, we'll continue to overcome any challenge."

*"In the face of adversity, it is our connections and resilience that light the way forward."*

# Chapter 11: Whispers of Doubt

*"Doubt is the seed of growth; when nurtured, it can lead to clarity and strength."*

As the team at Infinite Innovations prepared for the final stages of the American market launch, the pressure intensified. Long hours turned into sleepless nights, and the weight of their ambitions pressed heavily on everyone's shoulders. Despite their best efforts, whispers of doubt began to creep into the minds of even the most dedicated team members.

Ravi, while grateful for the support he received during his father's illness, felt a lingering sense of guilt for having left the team in a crucial phase. He often found himself questioning his decisions and abilities. Ananya, balancing the expectations of her family and the demands of her job, struggled to maintain her composure. The team's morale, once buoyant, began to waver under the relentless stress.

One afternoon, during a particularly tense meeting, Vikram noticed the strain on his team's faces. "Alright, everyone, let's take a break. We've been pushing ourselves hard, and it's starting to show. Take an hour to clear your heads, and we'll regroup."

As the team dispersed, Ravi and Ananya found themselves alone in the conference room. Ravi stared out the window, lost in thought. "Ananya, do you ever wonder if we're in over our heads?"

Ananya sighed, leaning back in her chair. "All the time. But we've come so far, Ravi. We can't back down now."

Ravi turned to her; his eyes filled with uncertainty. "I know, but sometimes it feels like no matter how hard we work, we're always one step behind."

Ananya reached out and placed a hand on his shoulder. "Ravi, we've faced tougher challenges before and come out stronger. We can do this. We just need to trust ourselves and each other."

Their conversation was interrupted by the arrival of Nikhil, who had overheard part of their discussion. "Hey, you two. Mind if I join you?"

Ravi nodded, and Nikhil took a seat. "I know things are tough right now," Nikhil began, "but I believe in what we're doing. We've got a great product, a great team, and the support of each other. Doubt is natural, but it doesn't define us."

Ravi and Ananya exchanged glances, feeling a renewed sense of determination. Nikhil's words, simple yet profound, reminded them of their shared purpose.

As the team reconvened, Vikram addressed them with a calm, reassuring tone. "I know we're all feeling the pressure, but we need to stay focused. Remember why we started this journey and the impact we aim to make. Let's tackle these final stages together."

Over the next few days, the team pushed forward with renewed vigor. They worked through weekends, refining their strategies and addressing last-minute issues. Despite the mounting stress, there was a palpable sense of camaraderie.

One evening, as the team worked late into the night, Ravi noticed Priya sitting alone, staring intently at her screen. He approached her, sensing something was wrong.

"Hey, Priya. Everything okay?" Ravi asked gently.

Priya looked up, her eyes weary. "I'm just worried, Ravi. We've put so much into this, and I'm scared it won't be enough."

Ravi sat down beside her. "I get it, Priya. We're all feeling the pressure. But we have to trust in our work and each other. We've come this far because of our dedication and teamwork. We can't lose sight of that now."

Priya nodded, a small smile forming on her lips. "Thanks, Ravi. I needed to hear that."

As the night wore on, the team continued to work tirelessly. The office buzzed with the hum of computers and the quiet murmur of discussions. Each member, despite their doubts and exhaustion, was driven by a shared goal.

In the days leading up to the launch, Ravi and Ananya made it a point to check in with each team member, offering words of encouragement and support. They knew that in moments of doubt, it was crucial to stay connected and uplifted.

On the eve of the launch, the team gathered in the conference room for one final meeting. Vikram stood before them, his expression one of pride and determination.

"We've faced countless challenges and overcome numerous obstacles to get here. This launch is a testament to our hard work, resilience, and unity. No matter what happens tomorrow, remember that we are a team. We've achieved something incredible together."

The room erupted in applause, the energy electric with anticipation and hope. Ravi and Ananya exchanged a glance, their earlier doubts replaced with a sense of calm confidence.

As the night turned into morning, the team made final preparations, their excitement tempered with a touch of nervousness. They knew that their journey was far from over, but they were ready to face whatever came next.

*"In moments of doubt, seek the strength within and the support around you; together, you can overcome any obstacle."*

## Chapter 12: The Launch

*"The culmination of effort and dreams is the spark that ignites the future."*

The day of the American market launch had finally arrived. The atmosphere in the office was electric, a blend of anticipation, excitement, and a touch of anxiety. The team at Infinite Innovations had poured their hearts and souls into this project, and now it was time to unveil their work to the world.

Ravi arrived early, the first one in the office. He took a moment to walk through the empty space, reflecting on the journey that had brought them to this point. Each desk, each room, held memories of late-night brainstorming sessions, moments of triumph, and the occasional setback. It was a testament to the team's resilience and dedication.

Ananya joined him shortly after, carrying a tray of coffee and breakfast pastries. "Thought we could all use a little fuel this morning," she said with a smile.

"Thanks, Ananya. This is exactly what we need," Ravi replied, taking a cup of coffee and savouring the warmth.

As the rest of the team trickled in, they gathered in the conference room for a final briefing. Vikram stood at the head of the table, his expression a mix of pride and determination.

"Today is the day we've been working towards for months. I want to thank each and every one of you for your hard work and dedication. We've faced challenges, but we've overcome them together. Now, it's time to show the world what we've created."

The team responded with a collective nod, their faces reflecting a blend of nervousness and excitement. They took their positions, ready to monitor the launch and respond to any immediate feedback.

The clock struck 9 AM, and with a few clicks, their product went live. There was a brief moment of silence, as if the world itself was holding its breath. Then, the first wave of user activity began to roll in.

Nikhil, who was monitoring the analytics, called out, "We've got our first users logging in. Feedback is coming in real-time."

Ravi and Ananya watched the screen intently, their hearts pounding. Every positive comment, every successful interaction, felt like a small victory. The initial feedback was encouraging, but they knew that the real test would be the sustained engagement and reception over the next few hours.

As the morning turned into afternoon, the team worked tirelessly to address any minor issues that arose. Priya and her customer support team were on high alert, responding to user queries and ensuring a smooth experience. Despite the intense pace, there was a palpable sense of camaraderie and shared purpose.

During a brief lull, Ananya approached Ravi, who was engrossed in monitoring the data. "How are you holding up?" she asked, handing him a bottle of water.

Ravi took the bottle and smiled. "I'm good. Just trying to stay on top of everything. How about you?"

Ananya shrugged, her eyes sparkling with a mix of excitement and exhaustion. "It's been a rollercoaster, but I think we're handling it well. The feedback has been mostly positive, which is a great sign."

They shared a moment of quiet satisfaction, knowing that their hard work was paying off. As the day progressed, the team settled into a rhythm, tackling challenges as they came and celebrating each success.

By evening, the initial surge had stabilized, and the overall feedback was overwhelmingly positive. The team's faces, though tired, were lit with pride and relief. They had done it. The American market launch was a success.

Vikram called everyone into the conference room for a final debrief. "I want to commend you all on an outstanding job today. We've achieved something remarkable, and it's all thanks to your dedication and teamwork. Let's take a moment to celebrate this milestone."

Ravi and Ananya exchanged a glance, a silent acknowledgment of the journey they had shared. The room filled with applause, cheers, and a few happy tears. It was a moment of triumph that they would all remember.

Later that evening, the team gathered at a nearby restaurant to celebrate their success. The mood was jubilant, a stark contrast to the tense anticipation of the morning.

Laughter and conversation filled the air as they enjoyed a well-deserved break.

At one point, Nikhil raised his glass. "To the best team anyone could ask for. We've faced challenges, but we've come out stronger. Here's to many more successes ahead."

"Cheers!" echoed around the table, glasses clinking in a toast to their collective effort and achievement.

As the night wore on, Ravi and Ananya found a quiet corner to reflect. "We did it, Ananya. We really did it," Ravi said, a note of wonder in his voice.

Ananya smiled, her eyes reflecting the city lights. "Yes, we did. And this is just the beginning.

There are still many challenges ahead, but I know we can face them together."

Ravi nodded, feeling a deep sense of gratitude. "To our team, to our future, and to the journey ahead."

They clinked their glasses, a silent promise of resilience and hope for whatever lay ahead.

*"Success is a journey marked by milestones of effort, resilience, and the courage to dream beyond the horizon."*

# Chapter 13: The Cost of Ambition

*"Ambition, when pursued relentlessly, can illuminate the path to success but also cast shadows on the soul."*

The high of the successful launch lingered in the office for a few days, but soon, the reality of the sustained effort required to maintain their momentum set in. The team knew they couldn't afford to rest on their laurels. While the initial feedback from the American market was overwhelmingly positive, it also brought new challenges and expectations.

Ravi found himself buried in data analytics, trying to identify trends and areas for improvement. The early successes were gratifying, but they needed to ensure long-term user engagement. The late nights continued, and he often found himself leaving the office only to see the sun rising.

Ananya was similarly consumed by her responsibilities. She had taken on the task of leading user experience enhancements, working closely with the design and development teams to implement changes based on user feedback. The work was intense, and the pressure to deliver swift results was immense.

As the days turned into weeks, the team began to feel the strain. Priya, juggling customer support and her own personal life, started to show signs of burnout. Nikhil, despite his usually calm demeanour, was often found pacing the office, his mind racing with new ideas and strategies.

One evening, as the office was bathed in the glow of computer screens, Ravi noticed Priya staring blankly at her monitor, her usual spark missing. He approached her, concerned.

"Priya, you look exhausted. When was the last time you took a break?" Ravi asked gently.

Priya forced a smile. "I'm fine, Ravi. Just a lot on my plate right now."

"Priya, I can see you're not fine. You need to take care of yourself. Why don't you take tomorrow off? We'll manage here," Ravi insisted.

Priya hesitated, then nodded reluctantly. "Maybe you're right. I could use a day to recharge."

Meanwhile, Ananya was dealing with her own struggles. The pressure from her family regarding marriage had not abated, and it was becoming increasingly difficult to balance their expectations with her demanding work schedule. One night, after another long day at the office, she returned home to find her mother waiting up for her.

"Ananya, we need to talk," her mother said, her tone serious.

"Amma, I'm really tired. Can this wait until tomorrow?" Ananya pleaded.

Her mother shook her head. "No, it can't. Your father and I are worried about you. You're working yourself to the bone, and you're not even considering your personal life. We've found a good match for you, and we want you to meet him."

Ananya felt a wave of frustration and helplessness. "Amma, I've told you before, I'm not ready for this right now. I'm committed to my work. Can't you understand that?"

Her mother's expression softened. "We understand, but we also want you to be happy and settled. Life is not just about work, Ananya."

Ananya sighed, feeling trapped. "I need time, Amma. Please, just give me some time."

As she retreated to her room, Ananya felt the weight of her dual responsibilities pressing down on her. The next day at the office, her usual focus was missing. Ravi noticed her distraction and decided to check in.

"Ananya, you seem a bit off today. Is everything alright?" Ravi asked, his voice filled with concern.

Ananya sighed, rubbing her temples. "It's my parents. They're pushing me about marriage again. It's just... a lot to handle."

Ravi nodded, understanding her predicament. "I'm sorry you're going through this, Ananya. If you need to take some time for yourself, please do. We'll manage."

"Thanks, Ravi. I appreciate it," Ananya replied, grateful for his understanding.

Despite the personal struggles, the team continued to push forward. However, the relentless pace was taking its toll. One evening, Vikram called an impromptu meeting.

"Everyone, I've noticed the strain we're all under," Vikram began, his tone serious but compassionate. "We've achieved something incredible, but we need to take care of ourselves. Starting next week, we're going to implement mandatory breaks and ensure everyone has time to recharge."

The team exchanged relieved glances. The acknowledgment of their efforts and the promise of rest was a much-needed balm.

That weekend, Ravi decided to visit his father, who was recovering well. The trip home was a welcome break from the constant grind. As he sat with his father, discussing the recent success and the pressures that came with it, Ravi found a sense of clarity.

"Appa, sometimes I wonder if all this ambition is worth the personal sacrifices," Ravi confessed. His father, a wise and experienced man, smiled gently. "Ravi, ambition is a powerful force, but it must be balanced with self-care and personal happiness. Success is important, but so is your well-being."

Ravi nodded, his father's words resonating deeply. "You're right, Appa. I need to find that balance."

Back in Bangalore, Ananya decided to take a day off to clear her mind. She visited a serene temple on the outskirts of the city, finding solace in the tranquil environment. As she sat in quiet contemplation, she realized the importance of taking care of her mental and emotional health.

Returning to the office with a renewed sense of purpose, Ananya felt more cantered. She approached Ravi, who seemed similarly recharged from his weekend at home.

"Ravi, I've been thinking. We need to set an example for the team. If we don't take care of ourselves, how can we expect them to do the same?" Ananya said.

Ravi nodded in agreement. "You're right, Ananya. Let's make self-care a priority for everyone, including ourselves."

With this new mindset, the team began to implement healthier work habits. Regular breaks, flexible working hours, and open discussions about stress and workload became the norm. The shift was gradual, but the positive impact was undeniable.

As they navigated the post-launch phase, the team at Infinite Innovations found a better balance between ambition and well-being. They continued to strive for excellence, but with a renewed understanding of the importance of self-care and personal happiness.

*"Balance in life is achieved not by prioritizing one aspect over another, but by finding harmony between ambition and well-being."*

# Chapter 14: Shadows of the Past

*"The past, when acknowledged, can illuminate the path forward and heal the unseen wounds."*

The new work-life balance at Infinite Innovations brought a sense of calm and rejuvenation to the team. However, the tranquillity was soon disrupted when Ravi received an unexpected message from an old friend, Aarav, who he hadn't spoken to in years.

"Ravi, it's been a while. Can we meet? There's something important I need to discuss with you," read the message.

Ravi was taken aback. Aarav had been his closest friend during his college days, but they had drifted apart after a falling out over a business venture that had gone sour. The message brought back a flood of memories, both good and bad.

Ravi debated whether to respond. The past was a Pandora's box he wasn't sure he wanted to open. But curiosity and a sense of unresolved business compelled him to agree. They arranged to meet at a quiet café in Koramangala.

When Ravi arrived, he saw Aarav sitting at a corner table, looking pensive. Aarav stood up as Ravi approached, a tentative smile on his face.

"Ravi, it's good to see you."

"You too, Aarav," Ravi replied, shaking his hand. They sat down, and an awkward silence followed.

Aarav broke the silence. "Ravi, I know it's been a long time, and we didn't part on the best of terms. But I've been following your work with Infinite Innovations. I'm impressed by what you've achieved."

"Thanks, Aarav. It hasn't been easy, but we're making progress," Ravi replied, still wary of where this conversation was heading.

Aarav took a deep breath. "I need to apologize for what happened back then. I handled things poorly, and I've regretted it ever since. I've wanted to make amends, but I didn't know how."

Ravi looked at him, the old wounds resurfacing but softened by time. "It was a tough time for both of us. We were young and ambitious. We made mistakes."

"I appreciate you saying that," Aarav said, visibly relieved. "I'm actually in a bit of a bind right now.

I started a new venture, but it's struggling. I could use some advice, maybe even some help."

Ravi was silent for a moment, contemplating. The idea of getting involved with Aarav again was daunting, but there was also a chance for redemption and closure. "Tell me more about it," he finally said.

As Aarav explained his business, Ravi found himself intrigued despite his initial reservations. They spent hours discussing strategies, market trends, and potential solutions. By the end of their meeting, Ravi felt a renewed sense of camaraderie with Aarav, though he remained cautious.

Back at the office, Ravi shared the encounter with Ananya. "It's strange, Ananya. Aarav and I have a lot of history. Helping him could be risky, but it also feels like the right thing to do."

Ananya listened thoughtfully. "Ravi, the past can be complicated. If helping Aarav feels right to you, then do it. But make sure it's for the right reasons, and set clear boundaries."

Ravi nodded, appreciating her perspective.

"You're right. I'll help him, but I'll be careful."

In the following weeks, Ravi found himself balancing his work at Infinite Innovations with advising Aarav. The added responsibility was challenging, but it also brought a sense of fulfilment. Aarav's venture began to show signs of improvement, and their renewed friendship flourished.

Meanwhile, at Infinite Innovations, Ananya and the team continued to refine their product and expand their user base. The initial success in the American market opened doors to new opportunities and partnerships. The team's morale was high, buoyed by their achievements and the healthier work environment.

One evening, as the team gathered for a celebratory dinner to mark another milestone, Ravi received a call from Aarav. "Ravi, I just wanted to thank you. Your advice has made a huge difference. I don't know how to repay you."

"You don't need to repay me, Aarav. Just keep pushing forward. We all deserve a second chance," Ravi replied, feeling a sense of closure he hadn't realized he needed.

The dinner was filled with laughter, stories, and a deep sense of camaraderie. Ananya, sitting next to Ravi, raised her glass for a toast. "To our journey, our growth, and the bonds we've formed along the way. Here's to many more successes together."

"Cheers!" the team echoed, clinking their glasses.

As the night wound down, Ravi and Ananya stepped outside for some fresh air. The city lights of Bangalore twinkled around them, a reflection of their own journey's bright spots and challenges.

"Ravi, I'm proud of what we've accomplished, both professionally and personally. It hasn't been easy, but it's been worth it," Ananya said, her voice filled with warmth.

Ravi smiled, feeling a deep sense of gratitude. "I couldn't have done it without you,

Ananya. Here's to facing whatever comes next, together."

*"The past, when embraced and understood, can be the foundation upon which we build a brighter future."*

# Chapter 15: Uncharted Waters

*"In uncharted waters, we discover the true depth of our courage and the boundless possibilities that lie beyond the horizon."*

With the American market launch deemed a success and the team's morale high, Infinite Innovations was riding a wave of optimism.

However, new challenges loomed on the horizon as they contemplated their next move. Expanding to new markets and sustaining growth required navigating uncharted waters.

During a Monday morning meeting, Vikram gathered the team to discuss future plans.

"We've achieved remarkable success in the American market, but we can't stop here. We need to explore new opportunities and continue to innovate. Let's brainstorm potential markets and strategies for our next expansion."

The team buzzed with excitement and ideas. Nikhil suggested exploring European markets, citing the tech-savvy population and robust infrastructure. Priya proposed looking into Asia, where rapid digitalization presented untapped potential. Ananya recommended enhancing their current offerings to create more value for existing users.

As ideas flowed, Ravi remained contemplative. He had been thinking deeply about their next steps and the potential risks involved. After everyone had shared their thoughts, he spoke up.

"All of these ideas are great, and I think we should pursue them. But we need to be strategic about it. Expanding too quickly without a solid foundation could backfire. We need to ensure our core product is robust and that we have the resources to support new ventures."

Vikram nodded in agreement. "Ravi's right. We need a balanced approach. Let's form smaller teams to focus on different aspects— market research, product enhancement, and resource allocation. We'll meet regularly to track our progress and make adjustments as needed."

The team divided into groups, each tasked with specific responsibilities. Ravi and Ananya led the product enhancement team, working on new features and improvements based on user feedback. Nikhil headed the market research team, delving into potential regions for expansion. Priya and her team focused on streamlining customer support and ensuring a seamless user experience.

As they delved into their tasks, the days grew longer, but the sense of purpose kept them motivated. One evening, while working late, Ravi and Ananya found themselves alone in the office.

"Ananya, do you ever worry that we might be stretching ourselves too thin?" Ravi asked, breaking the silence.

Ananya looked up from her screen, her eyes thoughtful. "Sometimes, yes. But I also believe in our ability to adapt and grow. We've faced challenges before and come out stronger. As long as we stay focused and support each other, I think we'll be okay."

Ravi nodded, reassured by her confidence. "You're right. We've got a great team and a solid plan. We just need to stay vigilant and be prepared for any obstacles."

As the weeks passed, the smaller teams made significant progress. Nikhil's research indicated that Europe, particularly Germany and the UK, presented the best opportunities for their next expansion. The tech-savvy population and favourable business environment made these markets attractive.

Meanwhile, Ravi and Ananya's team developed new features that enhanced user engagement and satisfaction.

They focused on personalization, allowing users to tailor their experience based on preferences and behaviour. The feedback was overwhelmingly positive, reinforcing their belief in the value of continuous innovation.

Priya's team streamlined customer support processes, reducing response times and improving user satisfaction. They implemented a new ticketing system and expanded their support team to handle the growing user base more efficiently.

With each team making strides, Vikram called another meeting to discuss their findings and next steps.

"Nikhil, your research on the European market is compelling. I think we should start planning our expansion there. Ravi and Ananya, your enhancements have significantly improved user satisfaction. Priya, your team's efforts in streamlining support are commendable. Let's put together a detailed plan for our European launch, focusing on Germany and the UK initially."

The team worked tirelessly to prepare for the new launch. They developed localized marketing strategies, partnered with local businesses, and ensured their product met regional regulations and standards. It was an intense period of preparation, but the team's synergy and dedication made it possible.

As the launch date approached, Ravi felt a familiar mix of excitement and anxiety. The lessons learned from their previous launch helped them avoid many pitfalls, but the uncertainty of a new market was still daunting.

On the eve of the launch, the team gathered for a final review. Vikram addressed them with a tone of calm confidence. "We've prepared thoroughly, and I have faith in each one of you. Let's give it our best shot and trust in our abilities. No matter the outcome, we'll learn and grow from this experience."

The room was filled with a quiet determination. They had come a long way, and now it was time to take another leap.

The next morning, as their product went live in Germany and the UK, the team held their breath, watching the initial reactions and user activity.

The feedback started trickling in, and to their relief, it was largely positive. Users appreciated the new features and the localized approach.

Ravi, monitoring the data, felt a surge of pride and relief. They had navigated the uncharted waters successfully. There were still challenges ahead, but they had proven their ability to adapt and thrive.

As the day came to an end, the team gathered to celebrate their achievement. The atmosphere was filled with a mix of exhaustion and exhilaration. Ananya raised her glass, echoing the sentiment of the entire team.

"To new beginnings, uncharted waters, and the courage to explore them together. Here's to our journey and the countless possibilities ahead."

"Cheers!" they all responded, their spirits high.

*"In every new venture, embrace the unknown with courage and curiosity; for it is in the uncharted waters that we discover our true potential."*

# Chapter 16: The Price of Progress

*"Every step forward comes with its own costs, but the true measure of progress is understanding and addressing those costs."*

The successful launch in Europe brought renewed energy and optimism to the team at Infinite Innovations. The feedback was overwhelmingly positive, and user engagement was on the rise. However, the relentless pace of work and the constant drive for excellence began to reveal its toll on the team.

Ravi, though proud of their achievements, started noticing the cracks in the team's morale. Late nights and high-pressure deadlines were becoming the norm again, despite their efforts to maintain a healthy work-life balance. The strain was visible on everyone's faces.

One morning, Ananya entered Ravi's office, her expression weary. "Ravi, we need to talk. The team is exhausted. We've been pushing hard for months, and it's starting to show."

Ravi nodded, knowing she was right. "I've noticed it too. We can't afford to burn out our best people. What do you suggest?"

Ananya sighed. "We need to slow down, at least for a bit. Give everyone a chance to recharge. Maybe even bring in some additional help to share the load."

Ravi agreed, and they took their concerns to Vikram. After a lengthy discussion, they decided to implement a mandatory break period for all employees. They also began the process of hiring additional staff to support their growing operations.

During this period of adjustment, Ravi found himself reflecting on the personal sacrifices he had made for the sake of the company. He missed spending time with his family and friends, and he knew he wasn't alone in feeling this way.

One weekend, Ravi decided to take a break and visit his old neighbourhood. Walking through the familiar streets, he felt a wave of nostalgia. He stopped by a local tea stall where he used to spend hours chatting with friends.

As he sipped his tea, Ravi spotted an old friend, Aditi, who he hadn't seen in years. She was sitting at a nearby table, engrossed in a book. Ravi approached her with a smile.

"Aditi, is that you?"

Aditi looked up, surprised. "Ravi! It's been ages.

How have you been?"

They caught up on their lives, reminiscing about old times. Aditi had become a successful writer, balancing her career with a fulfilling personal life. As they talked, Ravi realized how much he had missed the simple pleasures of life outside of work.

"Aditi, do you ever feel like you're sacrificing too much for your career?" Ravi asked, voicing the thoughts that had been on his mind.

Aditi nodded thoughtfully. "Sometimes, yes. But I've learned to set boundaries. Success is important, but so is living a balanced life. You have to find what works for you."

Ravi left their meeting feeling inspired. He knew he needed to make changes, not just for his team, but for himself as well.

Back at the office, the atmosphere was slowly improving. The mandatory breaks and new hires were helping to alleviate the pressure.

However, the financial strain of hiring additional staff and the cost of the European launch began to weigh on the company's finances.

Vikram called a meeting to address the issue. "We've made great strides, but our expenses are rising rapidly. We need to find ways to increase our revenue without compromising our team's well-being."

The team brainstormed various ideas, from introducing premium features to exploring new markets. Ananya suggested expanding their partnership network, leveraging existing relationships to create new revenue streams.

As they implemented these strategies, Ravi took a more active role in mentoring the new hires, ensuring they integrated smoothly into the team. He also made a conscious effort to reconnect with his own life outside of work, spending more time with his family and friends.

One evening, as the sun set over Bangalore, Ravi and Ananya sat on the office terrace, reflecting on the journey so far.

"Ananya, do you ever wonder if we're doing the right thing?" Ravi asked, his voice tinged with uncertainty.

Ananya smiled; her eyes thoughtful. "I think we are, Ravi. But it's important to remember that progress comes with challenges. The key is to address them without losing sight of what truly matters."

Ravi nodded, feeling a renewed sense of purpose. "You're right. We've built something incredible here, but we need to ensure it doesn't come at the cost of our well-being."

The following weeks saw a gradual improvement in the team's morale and productivity. The new revenue strategies started to bear fruit, easing the financial strain. The office buzzed with a healthier, more sustainable energy.

As they navigated these changes, Ravi and Ananya remained committed to fostering a supportive work environment. They held regular check-ins with the team, encouraging open communication and addressing concerns promptly.

One day, during a team meeting, Priya spoke up. "I just wanted to say thank you for the changes we've made. It's made a big difference for all of us."

Her words were met with nods of agreement and smiles from the team. It was a small but significant victory, a reminder that they were on the right path.

*"Progress is not only about moving forward but also about taking care of those who walk the journey with you."*

# Chapter 17: The Whisper of Doubt

*"Doubt is the whisper that challenges our resolve; facing it is the first step toward true growth."*

With the team at Infinite Innovations finding a healthier rhythm, the office environment became more vibrant. The new hires integrated well, and the increased revenue streams stabilized the financial situation. However, amidst this newfound stability, Ravi began experiencing a whisper of doubt, a nagging feeling that perhaps they were missing something crucial.

One evening, Ravi stayed late at the office, sifting through user feedback and market trends. The data was positive, but something didn't sit right with him. He couldn't shake the feeling that their product, while successful, had reached a plateau.

Ananya noticed his preoccupation over the next few days. During a casual chat in the break room, she approached him. "Ravi, you seem distracted lately. Is everything okay?"

Ravi sighed, rubbing his temples. "I don't know, Ananya. Something feels off. We're doing well, but I can't help feeling like we're stagnating. What if we're missing something important?"

Ananya looked thoughtful. "I understand that feeling. Maybe it's time we took a step back and re-evaluated our vision and strategy. Sometimes, the best way to move forward is to reassess where we stand."

Taking her advice to heart, Ravi called for a strategy retreat. The entire team would spend a weekend away from the office to brainstorm, reflect, and realign their goals. They chose a serene resort on the outskirts of Bangalore, hoping the change of scenery would inspire fresh ideas.

At the retreat, the atmosphere was relaxed but focused. Vikram kicked off the sessions with a simple question: "What do we want Infinite Innovations to stand for in the next five years?"

The question sparked a lively discussion. Nikhil emphasized the importance of staying ahead of technological trends. Priya highlighted the need for continued focus on user experience and satisfaction. Ananya proposed exploring new product lines to diversify their offerings.

As they delved deeper, Ravi encouraged everyone to think outside the box. "We've built something amazing, but innovation means constantly evolving. Let's push ourselves to think bigger."

The team broke into smaller groups for workshops, each tasked with tackling different aspects of their business. Ravi and Ananya led a session on potential new technologies, while Nikhil and Priya focused on market expansion strategies.

During these sessions, Ravi couldn't help but notice a recurring theme: sustainability. Many team members expressed a desire to incorporate eco-friendly practices into their operations and products. This idea resonated with Ravi. He had always believed in the importance of creating a positive impact, but they had yet to explore this avenue seriously.

On the final day of the retreat, the team reconvened to share their insights and proposals. The discussions were invigorating, filled with innovative ideas and ambitious goals. One idea that stood out was the development of a new product line focused on sustainability—

technology that not only served users but also contributed to a greener planet.

Vikram was enthusiastic about the proposal. "This could set us apart in the market and align with a growing global consciousness. Let's explore this further."

Back at the office, the team threw themselves into research and development. They collaborated with experts in sustainable technology, seeking ways to integrate eco-friendly practices into their existing products and exploring new ones.

Ravi, fuelled by a renewed sense of purpose, led the charge. He worked closely with the R&D team, ensuring their innovations were not only groundbreaking but also environmentally responsible. The process was challenging, requiring them to rethink many aspects of their operations, but the team's passion and commitment drove them forward.

As the weeks turned into months, the office buzzed with excitement over the new direction. The first prototype of their sustainable product—a smart home device that optimized energy usage—was met with enthusiastic approval from testers. The feedback was promising, and the team felt a sense of pride and accomplishment.

One evening, Ravi and Ananya sat on the office terrace, reflecting on the journey so far.

"Ananya, this new direction feels right. We're not just innovating; we're making a positive impact," Ravi said, his voice filled with conviction.

Ananya smiled, her eyes shining with shared excitement. "I agree. This is about more than just business. It's about creating something meaningful."

Their conversation was interrupted by a call from Vikram. He had just received news from a potential investor interested in their sustainable technology. The investor, impressed by their vision and prototype, wanted to meet and discuss a significant partnership.

The team prepared meticulously for the meeting, determined to make a strong impression. When the day arrived, they presented their vision with passion and clarity. The investor, a prominent figure in the tech industry, was not only impressed by their product but also by their commitment to sustainability.

"I believe in what you're doing here," the investor said. "This is the future of technology. I'm excited to partner with Infinite Innovations and support your journey."

The partnership brought a surge of resources and opportunities, propelling their sustainable technology initiatives forward. The team's hard work and dedication were paying off, and they felt a renewed sense of purpose.

As they celebrated this milestone, Ravi couldn't help but reflect on the journey. The whisper of doubt had led them to re-evaluate and innovate, resulting in a path that felt both exciting and meaningful.

*"Embrace doubt as a catalyst for growth, for it often leads us to uncover our true potential and purpose."*

## Chapter 18: Ripples of Innovation

*"Innovation is the pebble that creates ripples, changing the landscape one wave at a time."*

The partnership with the prominent investor brought a whirlwind of activity to Infinite Innovations. With increased resources and visibility, the team found themselves in the spotlight. The smart home device, their flagship sustainable product, was set to launch, and the anticipation was palpable.

The days leading up to the launch were a blur of final tests, marketing preparations, and strategy meetings. Ravi, while exhilarated, felt the pressure mounting. He was determined to ensure everything went smoothly.

One evening, as he worked late in the office, he received a message from Aarav. They had stayed in touch, and Aarav's venture was now thriving thanks to Ravi's guidance.

"Ravi, I heard about the new product launch. Congratulations! I'd love to catch up and hear more about it," the message read.

Ravi smiled, grateful for the support. He replied, setting up a meeting for the weekend.

Aarav had become a close friend again, and their renewed bond was a source of strength for Ravi.

The weekend arrived, and Ravi met Aarav at their favourite café in Koramangala. The place was buzzing with activity, a stark contrast to the calm Ravi sought. Still, it was the perfect spot to unwind.

"Aarav, it's good to see you," Ravi greeted, sitting down with a sigh of relief.

"You too, Ravi. So, tell me all about this new product. I've been following your progress, and it sounds groundbreaking."

Ravi delved into the details of the smart home device, explaining its features and the team's commitment to sustainability. Aarav listened intently, his eyes reflecting admiration and curiosity.

"Ravi, this is incredible. You're not just innovating; you're making a real impact. It's inspiring," Aarav said, his voice filled with genuine admiration.

Their conversation shifted to personal matters, and Ravi found himself sharing the challenges and triumphs of the past months.

Aarav, in turn, spoke about his own journey, the ups and downs of rebuilding his business.

As they parted ways, Ravi felt a renewed sense of determination. The conversation with Aarav had reminded him of the importance of their work and the potential to create lasting change. Back at the office, the final preparations for the launch were in full swing.

The team worked seamlessly, each member contributing their expertise to ensure every detail was perfect. Ananya coordinated the marketing strategy, while Nikhil handled the technical aspects. Priya managed customer support, ensuring they were prepared for the influx of inquiries.

The launch day arrived, and the atmosphere was electric. The office was filled with excitement and nervous energy. They had invited media, potential customers, and industry leaders to the event, hoping to make a strong impression.

Vikram addressed the gathering, his voice confident and inspiring. "Today marks a significant milestone for Infinite Innovations. We are proud to introduce our smart home device, a product that not only enhances your life but also contributes to a sustainable future. Our journey has been driven by a commitment to innovation and responsibility, and we are excited to share this with the world."

Ravi and Ananya took the stage next, demonstrating the features of the device and highlighting its eco-friendly benefits. The audience was captivated, and the feedback was overwhelmingly positive. The event was a success, and the team's hard work had paid off.

In the following weeks, the smart home device received rave reviews and high demand. The success of the launch propelled Infinite Innovations into a new phase of growth. They expanded their team, investing in research and development to further enhance their products.

One evening, Ravi and Ananya sat in the now-familiar terrace, reflecting on their journey.

"Ananya, can you believe how far we've come? From our initial struggles to launching a product that's making a real impact—it's surreal," Ravi said, his voice filled with awe.

Ananya smiled, her eyes reflecting the same sentiment. "It is. But it's also a testament to our team's dedication and vision. We believed in what we were doing, and we made it happen."

Ravi nodded, feeling a deep sense of gratitude. "I'm proud of what we've achieved, but I'm even more excited about what lies ahead. There's so much potential, so many possibilities."

As they sat there, watching the city lights twinkle around them, they felt a sense of accomplishment and anticipation. The ripples of their innovation were spreading, creating waves of change that would shape the future.

*"Innovation doesn't end with a single success; it's the continuous ripple effect that transforms the world."*

# Chapter 19: Shifting Tides

*"In the ebb and flow of success, it's the ability to adapt that defines true resilience."*

The success of the smart home device had catapulted Infinite Innovations into a new realm of possibilities. With increased visibility and market demand, the company found itself navigating the complexities of rapid growth. The challenge now was to sustain their momentum while staying true to their core values.

Ravi, Ananya, Vikram, and the rest of the leadership team gathered for a strategic meeting. The atmosphere was a mix of excitement and urgency as they discussed the future direction of the company.

Vikram started the meeting with an overview of their current status. "We've achieved remarkable success with our smart home device, but we need to be mindful of the challenges that come with rapid growth. Our focus should be on scaling sustainably and exploring new opportunities without losing sight of our vision."

Nikhil chimed in. "Our user base is expanding quickly, and we need to ensure our infrastructure can handle the increased demand. We should also look into enhancing our data security measures to protect our users' information."

Priya added, "Customer support will be critical. We need to expand our team and improve our processes to maintain high levels of satisfaction."

Ananya, always the strategist, brought up the need for diversification. "We should explore new product lines and markets. Innovation has been our strength, and we need to leverage it to create a broader portfolio."

Ravi listened, taking in everyone's perspectives. He felt a renewed sense of purpose, ready to tackle the challenges ahead. "I agree with all of you. Let's break into smaller teams and focus on these key areas. We'll reconvene regularly to track our progress and make adjustments as needed."

The team divided into focus groups, each with specific objectives. Ravi led the product development team, tasked with creating new innovative solutions. Ananya took charge of market expansion, exploring potential regions and strategies. Nikhil focused on strengthening their infrastructure and data security, while Priya spearheaded customer support enhancements.

As the weeks passed, the office buzzed with activity. The product development team brainstormed and tested new ideas, driven by Ravi's leadership. They explored various concepts, from advanced home automation to AI-driven personal assistants, aiming to stay ahead of market trends.

Meanwhile, Ananya's market expansion team conducted extensive research, identifying promising regions for growth. They focused on Asia and Latin America, regions with emerging markets and increasing digital adoption. They crafted localized marketing strategies and established partnerships with local businesses to ease entry.

Nikhil's team worked tirelessly to upgrade their infrastructure, implementing robust data security measures and ensuring their systems could handle the growing user base. They also explored cutting-edge technologies to enhance performance and reliability.

Priya's team expanded the customer support division, hiring and training new staff to provide exceptional service. They introduced advanced support tools, streamlined processes, and established a 24/7 support system to cater to global users.

Despite the intense workload, the team's camaraderie and shared vision kept morale high. Late nights and weekend brainstorming sessions became common, but the sense of purpose made it all worthwhile.

One evening, Ravi and Ananya found themselves in the office, reflecting on their progress.

"Ananya, it's incredible to see how far we've come. The team's dedication is inspiring," Ravi said, his voice filled with pride.

Ananya nodded, her eyes shining with determination. "It is. But we must stay vigilant. Rapid growth brings its own set of challenges, and we need to be prepared."

Ravi agreed. "Absolutely. We need to stay agile and adaptable, ready to pivot when necessary."

As they spoke, a notification pinged on Ravi's phone. It was an email from Vikram, marked urgent. He opened it and read through quickly, his expression shifting to one of concern.

"Ananya, we need to address this immediately. It's a potential security breach. Nikhil and his team need to be informed right away."

They rushed to Nikhil's office, finding him deep in a discussion with his team. Ravi explained the situation, and Nikhil sprang into action, coordinating efforts to investigate and mitigate the breach.

The following hours were tense as the team worked around the clock to secure their systems and identify the source of the breach. The incident was a stark reminder of the vulnerabilities that came with their growth and the importance of maintaining stringent security measures.

By dawn, the immediate threat was contained, and the team breathed a collective sigh of relief. Ravi addressed the exhausted but relieved group.

"This incident has highlighted the importance of vigilance. We've handled it well, but we need to ensure we have even stronger measures in place moving forward. Thank you for your hard work and dedication."

The team's resilience was commendable, but the experience left a lasting impact. They doubled down on security protocols, conducted comprehensive audits, and implemented advanced threat detection systems.

As they navigated these challenges, the importance of their mission and the impact of their work became even clearer. They were not just building products; they were shaping the future.

*"Resilience is not just about weathering storms but learning from them to build stronger foundations."*

# Chapter 20: Reflections and New Beginnings

*"The journey of innovation is endless, but every milestone is a reminder of how far we've come and the endless possibilities ahead."*

The incident with the security breach had been a wake-up call for Infinite Innovations, reinforcing the importance of vigilance and resilience. With their systems fortified and their team more united than ever, the company continued to thrive, pushing the boundaries of technology and sustainability.

Months passed, and the company saw unprecedented growth. Their product lines expanded, their user base grew exponentially, and their reputation as pioneers in sustainable technology solidified. Yet, amid the success, Ravi and his team never lost sight of their core values—innovation, responsibility, and balance.

One evening, as the office hummed with the energy of another successful day, Ravi called for a company-wide meeting. The room filled with the familiar faces of colleagues who had become like family over the years. There was an air of anticipation as Ravi stood before them, a mixture of pride and nostalgia in his eyes.

"Today marks a significant milestone for us," Ravi began, his voice steady and warm. "We've achieved remarkable things together. From our humble beginnings to where we stand now, it's been an incredible journey. But today, I want to reflect on something more personal—the people behind the innovation, the heart and soul of Infinite Innovations."

He looked around the room, making eye contact with many of his team members. "Ananya, you've been my partner in this journey from the start. Your strategic brilliance and unwavering support have been invaluable. Vikram, your leadership has guided us through the toughest challenges. Nikhil, your technical expertise has been the backbone of our products. Priya, your dedication to our customers has ensured we remain trusted and loved."

Ravi paused, his eyes misting slightly. "And to every single one of you, thank you. This success belongs to all of us. We've built more than a company; we've built a community."

The room erupted in applause, and Ananya stepped forward, taking Ravi's hand. "Ravi, we couldn't have asked for a better leader. Your vision and compassion have driven us to achieve things we once only dreamed of."

As the applause died down, Ravi continued, "But our journey doesn't end here. Innovation is an endless path. We will continue to push boundaries, explore new horizons, and create a better future for our planet. The challenges will come, but so will the triumphs. Together, we will rise to meet them."

The meeting ended with a sense of renewed purpose and excitement for the future. The team gathered for a celebratory dinner, sharing stories, laughter, and dreams for what lay ahead.

Later that night, Ravi found himself on the office terrace, the city lights of Bangalore shimmering in the distance. Ananya joined him, and they stood in comfortable silence, reflecting on their journey.

"Do you remember when we started this, Ananya?" Ravi asked, his voice soft with nostalgia. "We had so many dreams, so much ambition. It's incredible to see how far we've come."

Ananya nodded, her gaze steady. "I remember, Ravi. And I also remember the challenges, the late nights, the doubts. But we believed in our vision and in each other. That's what got us here."

Ravi smiled. "And that's what will keep us moving forward. This journey has taught me that success is not just about innovation or profits. It's about the people, the relationships we build, and the positive impact we make."

As they stood there, a sense of peace washed over them. The future was uncertain, but it was also full of endless possibilities.

The next morning, the team gathered for their regular strategy meeting, but there was an air of excitement as they discussed new projects and ideas. Ravi felt a sense of fulfilment, knowing they were not just reacting to change but driving it.

A few weeks later, the company announced their latest initiative: a scholarship program for young innovators from underprivileged backgrounds. The program aimed to nurture the next generation of tech leaders, providing them with the resources and support they needed to succeed.

The response was overwhelming. Applications poured in from across the country, and the team worked tirelessly to select the most promising candidates. The scholarship recipients, full of hope and ambition, were welcomed into the Infinite Innovations family.

At the inaugural event for the scholarship program, Ravi addressed the young innovators. "You are the future. Your ideas, your passion, your creativity—these are the things that will drive progress. We are here to support you, to mentor you, and to learn from you. Together, we will continue to push the boundaries of what's possible."

The applause was thunderous, and as Ravi looked out at the bright faces before him, he felt a deep sense of fulfilment. This was the legacy of Infinite Innovations—a commitment to progress, a dedication to sustainability, and a belief in the power of people to change the world.

*"The end of one journey is the beginning of another. Embrace the possibilities, cherish the memories, and always strive to make a difference."*

\*\*\*\*\*\*\*

Pugal *Yazhini*

\*\*\*\*\*\*\*

**Life** is a **Journey**

*THE END*

**Love** and **Live**

.

9 798224 081592